Swimming Pool Summer

REBECCA FARNWORTH

arrow books

Published by Arrow Books, 2013

2 4 6 8 10 9 7 5 3 1

Addr… …imited

ISBN 9780099564478

The Random House Group Limited supports the Forest Stewardship Council® (FSC®), the leading international forest-certification organisation. Our books carrying the FSC label are printed on FSC®-certified paper. FSC is the only forest-certification scheme supported by the leading environmental organisations, including Greenpeace. Our paper procurement policy can be found at: www.randomhouse.co.uk/environment

MIX
Paper from responsible sources
FSC www.fsc.org FSC® C016897

Typeset by SX Composing DTP, Rayleigh, Essex
Printed and bound by CPI Group (UK) Ltd, Croydon, CR0 4YY